For my mother —B.W.·

JACOB & WILHELM GRIMM

JORINDA
and
JORINDEL

Retold and illustrated by

BERNADETTE WATTS

NORTH-SOUTH BOOKS
NEW YORK · LONDON

Once upon a time, deep in
the middle of a forest, stood
an old castle. An ancient
witch lived in the castle.

By day she fluttered about
disguised as an owl or slunk
around as a cat.

But at sunset she always turned into an old woman again.

If any young man, walking in the forest, came within one hundred steps of the castle he became spellbound and could not move until the witch came and set him free, which she would not do until he promised never to return.

But if a young girl came too near, the witch turned her into a bird and locked her in a cage that she hung in the castle. There were seven hundred cages hanging in the castle, each with a beautiful bird inside.

Now there was a maiden called Jorinda who was
the prettiest of all the pretty girls. A shepherd boy
called Jorindel loved her greatly and soon the two
of them were to marry. One evening they walked
together in the forest.

"We must be careful not to go too near the old
    fairy's castle," said Jorindel.

It was a beautiful evening. The last rays of the
setting sun fell between the slender trees and across
the fragrant undergrowth. Turtledoves cooed from
the tall birch trees.

Jorinda sat down to gaze at the sunset and Jorindel sat down beside her. They both felt sad but did not understand why. They felt they were about to be parted from one another forever. They had walked such a long way that when they looked around for the path home they discovered that they were lost.

The sun was now falling fast and half its circle had disappeared behind the hill.

Suddenly something startled Jorindel. He looked behind him and saw through the bushes that they had come too close to the castle walls. He trembled with fear.

Jorinda was singing—

> "The ringdove sang from the willow-spray,
> Well-a-day! Well-a-day!
> He mourned the fate of his darling mate,
> Well-a-day!"

But her song stopped suddenly. Jorinda had been turned into a nightingale. Her song faded away mournfully.

An owl with fiery eyes circled round three times. And three times the owl shrieked, *Tu-whu! Tu-whu! Tu-whu!* Jorindel was transfixed. He could not cry or speak or move.

Then the sun sank below the horizon. Night fell, and the horrible owl flew into a bush. But a moment later the old witch appeared, pale and bony, with staring eyes and a nose and chin that almost met. She seized the nightingale and hobbled away.

Poor Jorindel could do nothing for he could not move from the spot.

At last the ugly witch returned and sang hoarsely—

> "Till the prisoner is fast,
> And her doom is cast,
> There stay! Oh stay!
> When the charm is around her,
> And the spell has bound her,
> Go away! Go away!"

Suddenly Jorindel was free. He begged the witch to give him back his sweetheart. She only cackled and said, "You will never see her again." She then disappeared into the darkness.

Jorindel prayed and wept and grieved. "Alas," he cried, "what will become of me?" Heartbroken, he could not bear to go home but went instead to a strange village where he found work keeping sheep.

Many times he walked in the enchanted forest as close to the castle as he dared. But he never heard or saw Jorinda.

After some time he had a dream where he found a beautiful purple flower and in the heart of the flower lay a lustrous pearl. He dreamed that he plucked the flower and carried it to the castle. Then he went inside and everything that he touched with the flower was freed from enchantment. And so he rescued Jorinda.

Jorindel awoke the next morning full of hope. He searched, without rest, through hills and dales for the beautiful flower. For eight days he searched in vain. Then at daybreak on the ninth day he found it, and in the heart of the deep purple petals lay a large dewdrop, as lustrous as a pearl.

Jorindel plucked the flower, then walked, night and day, until he came to the castle.

He walked quite near to the walls but was not transfixed as he was before. He crept right up to the entrance. When he touched the doors with the flower they sprang open. He entered and crossed a courtyard, listening to the songs of hundreds of birds.

Jorindel followed the sounds to where the witch sat with seven hundred birds singing in seven hundred cages. When the witch saw Jorindel she screamed with rage. But she could not come anywhere near him for the magic flower he carried kept him safe.

Jorindel gazed at all the birds, but there were so many nightingales that he did not know which one was Jorinda.

While he was wondering what to do he caught sight of the witch taking down one of the cages and hurrying toward the door. Jorindel sprang after her.

Jorindel touched the cage with the flower. And there was Jorinda standing before him. She threw her arms around his neck, looking as pretty as she had when they had walked together in the forest.

Jorindel then touched all the other cages with the flower so that the birds became young girls again.

Jorindel and Jorinda returned to their
own village where they were married. They
lived happily together for many years.
And so did many other lads and their
sweethearts who had been enchanted
by the old witch.

Copyright © 2005 by Bernadette Watts
First published in Switzerland under the title *Jorinde und Joringel*
by NordSüd Verlag AG, Gossau Zürich, Switzerland

All rights reserved. No part of this book may be reproduced or utilized in
any form or by any means, electronic or mechanical, including photocopying,
recording, or any information storage and retrieval system, without
permission in writing from the publisher.

First published in the United States, Great Britain, Canada,
Australia, and New Zealand in 2005 by North-South Books,
an imprint of NordSüd Verlag AG, Gossau Zürich, Switzerland.
Distributed in the United States by North-South Books Inc., New York.

Library of Congress Cataloging-in-Publication Data is available.
A CIP catalogue record for this book is available from The British Library.
ISBN 0-7358-1987-4 (trade edition) 10 9 8 7 6 5 4 3 2 1
ISBN 0-7358-1988-2 (library edition) 10 9 8 7 6 5 4 3 2 1
Color separations by Art4site, England. Printed in Belgium
For more information about our books, and the authors and artists
who create them, visit our web site: www.northsouth.com